Only a Summer

Kasper Ridge - Prequel

Delancey Stewart

Contents

Follow Delancey!

Don't miss sneak peaks and a FREE bonus story when you sign up for my newsletter here!

Just click the link or point your browser to https://geni. us/Delancey-friends

Or scan the QR code now!

Chapter One

WILEY

"It's not you, it's me."

They were the words no one in a serious relationship ever wanted to hear, much less from his fiancée. But if I was honest, they weren't exactly breaking my heart.

Amberlynn's face was streaked with tears as we sat on the porch swing at her mother's house after Sunday dinner, and I took her hand in mine, a deep aching sadness rising inside me at the loss of something I'd known a long time, even though I'd also known for a while it wasn't right.

"Amberlynn," I said, uncertain what words would express my complete agreement that we were definitely not cut out for marriage, but which would also tell her that I was sad about it. Historically, words were not my strong suit.

"Don't say anything," she said, shaking her head. *Thank God.*

"I can't bear it. I've known you my whole life, Wiley. Loved you just as long."

"Well, I mean, not when we were little. Like, not when we were toddlers," I pointed out.

She pulled her hand out of mine and frowned at me. "Doesn't this make you sad at all? You were my high school sweetheart. And it's over." Tears rolled down her pretty face, streaking the makeup around her eyes.

Amber was beautiful—she always had been. She was the ultimate girl's girl, and maybe that was part of the problem. I wasn't the most refined of men. I tried, but I'd never really been what she wanted, never really made it to the level of sophistication she seemed to require. And to be honest? It was a relief to be off the hook, even though I'd miss the sweet familiarity of our long-time relationship.

"Amber, honey!" Lottie Tanner appeared on the darkened porch, coming out the screen door and wiping her hands on her apron. "Oh, there you two are. I was beginning to worry you'd snuck back out to the gazebo again for some—"

"Mom!" Amber sniffled.

"Oh dear," Lottie said, clearly realizing all was not well here as she took in Amber's tears. "Oh no, what's happened?"

"We broke up," Amber said, wailing the words, which led Lottie to shoot me a scathing look.

"It was mutual," I said, hoping to avoid being swatted about the ears with a wooden spoon, something Lottie had done once in high school when I'd told Amber I thought we should take a break and she'd gone home to tell Lottie what an ass I was.

Lottie sat on the porch swing next to Amberlynn, which made the whole contraption wobble and groan. I worried for a moment that it might fall, thinking back to the time when I'd hung the thing out here, my senior year in high school. Had I remembered to use anchor bolts? Surely it would have fallen before now if not.

Amber leaned into her mother's side, and as Lottie wrapped her youngest daughter in her arms, I knew without question that this was the right thing. Amberlynn was amazing, and so was the whole Tanner family. But it wasn't right for me.

"I love you. Both of you," I told them. "And I probably always will. But I think this is the right thing. We were so young when we got engaged . . ."

"It's okay, Wiley," Amber sniffed, her voice barely audible from where her mouth was smashed against Lottie's shoulder. "Mom, let go!"

Lottie released her and wiped at her own face. "Oh, you two." She took a deep breath and then stood back up, sending another shudder through the swing. "Maybe it's for the best, though. Maybe this is the mature thing to do." She sniffed. "Still, I was really hoping for a wedding."

"Mom," Amberlynn said, sounding much less upset now. "Paige and Addie are both engaged. You'll get your wedding."

Lottie nodded and then turned to me. "Wiley."

I stood, realizing she was essentially summoning me to face her. I wasn't sure if the swat was about to arrive, but she wasn't holding a spoon, so I decided to be brave. "Mrs. Tanner."

Then she surprised me by throwing her arms around me and pulling me against her fiercely. She was so short that her spray-fixed silver bob barely came to my chest, but I hugged her back. She'd been my mom too for most of my life, since my own mother had died when I was young.

"You always have a home here, Wiley, whether you and Amberlynn are getting married or not. We all love you." She squeezed me tight and then let me go.

"Thank you," I said, swallowing a surprising lump in my throat. "That means a lot to me." It did. And I realized then that maybe part of the reason I'd stayed with Amberlynn so long was because it was hard to give up the family I'd found here, with the Tanners. "I love you guys too," I said.

"Don't be a stranger," Lottie told me, and I realized it was time for me to go.

Amberlynn stood and hugged me again, and I felt my heart release. "Bye," I told her, already missing everything that had made up my life for the last twelve years. But it was the right thing. And I'd probably already stayed too long.

I drove to the distillery, needing the familiar tasks of work to keep my body busy while my mind and heart processed the sudden shift in my life.

"Can't get enough, eh?" Wade joked when he stepped in to find me checking dates on the whiskey aging in the barrel room.

My twin brother ran the bar that was connected to the distillery, so it was no surprise to find him here on a Sunday night. He also lived above the place, in the apartment he shared with his girlfriend, Veronica.

"Yeah, just needed to think."

"Uh oh." He faced me, waiting.

"We broke up."

Wade let out a long, low whistle. "You okay?"

My brother wasn't the emotional type—neither of us was—but he and I had been together our whole lives and I didn't have to say much for him to know exactly what was going on.

"Yeah, actually. Maybe it's past time."

He nodded. "I'm here if you need me."

"Yeah, thanks. Just need to process, you know? Figure out what's next."

"Drink?" he asked, picking up two bottles of the Half Cat Whiskey we were famous for to carry back over to the bar. "Just closing up and restocking."

"Yeah," I agreed, following him back through the entrance hallway that divided the distillery and the bar. Mr. FluffyNuts, our cat, was wheeling his way across the floor when I came in, but he detoured to come say hello, his little wheelchair squeaking as he dragged his back half with his front paws.

I knelt down to pet him. "Hey little guy, how are you? We need to get this chair oiled for you, don't we?"

"I like it squeaky," Wade said, pouring a couple fingers of whiskey into a glass behind the bar. "I always know where he is."

Our half cat was a rescue, and though he was a little disheveled and unconventional as pets went, he fit us pretty well and we gave him a good home here. Plus, he was the inspiration for our artisan whiskey.

I slid onto a stool and touched my glass to my brother's. After a sip, he put his glass down and turned to pick something up from the counter behind him. "Almost forgot. You got a call earlier."

"Yeah?"

"Remember Archie Kasper from high school?" He waved a slip of paper in his hand. Wade and I had both been good friends with a kid whose dad was in the military here for a bit. He'd been here until our junior year and then moved away.

"Yeah," I said. "He called?"

"Yep. Wanted to see if you felt like delivering some Half Cat out to some fancy resort he's got going in Colorado."

"Colorado," I said, the word rolling off my tongue as my mind turned the idea of a trip over in my mind. "What else did he say?"

"Just give him a call." He handed me the number. My brother leaned across the bar on his elbows and eyed me. "You thinking a trip might be a good plan?"

"I guess I'll see what he has in mind." I pulled my phone from my pocket. It was two hours earlier in Colorado, so I figured it wouldn't be too late.

"Hello?" A voice picked up after two rings.

"Kasper?" I said. "Wiley Blanchard."

"Hey Coyote, how the hell are you?" His voice was jovial, every bit as good-natured as I remembered, though I knew the guy had been through some rough times since I'd seen him last as kids.

"Good," I said. "Well, I mean, maybe I've been better, actually. Just broke up with Amberlynn."

"Your high school girlfriend?"

"Yeah. We got engaged after she finished college. It's been four years now."

"Long relationship. Long engagement," he said.

"Maybe a sign of something I should have seen a while ago," I admitted.

"I remember her. Pretty girl."

"She still is. Great family, too."

"Sorry, man," he said. "That's rough. But maybe the timing is good then. I was hoping I might be able to convince you and your brother to come out here, maybe sell me some of that hooch you've been making out there."

"Not hooch," I corrected. "Half Cat is *premium* whiskey." I wiggled my eyebrows at my brother. This was a hill I was willing to die on.

"Of course it is," he laughed. "But your brother already told me he's too whipped for a road trip."

"He is." I grinned at Wade, who was busily texting his girlfriend. She lived here half the time and spent the other half at her winery in Virginia, and my brother was well and truly whipped.

"But maybe you'd be interested in an extended vacation in the Rockies?"

"What's going on?" I asked.

Kasper told me a long story about his uncle dying and leaving some mountain resort in Colorado to him and his sister. "The place is in rough shape," he said. "But we're going to make a go of it. My uncle was a little bit eccentric.

He left some crazy treasure maps and shit, along with a ton of debt. But I think there's something here, and I want to get the place going again."

"Is it a ski resort?" I asked.

"It will be. We're going to start with summer operations, and my sister the mountain man has some crazy yurt plan she's setting up. But we'll need a stocked bar at the very least."

"Of course," I agreed, trying to remember if I knew Kasper's sister. I couldn't picture her, but she'd been a few years younger. She sounded a little scary, based on his mountain man description.

"So we'll feature Half Cat as our *premium* whiskey of choice. Spend your summer out here with me, man. You can run the bar, help me figure out what else to stock and maybe toss in some manual labor while you're at it."

"You know what?" I said, the idea taking root inside me and relieving some of the uncomfortable feelings of detachment I'd had since leaving Amberlynn's. "That sounds perfect."

We made arrangements, and I hung up.

"So you're leaving the nest?" Wade asked, turning back to me.

"Just for the summer," I said. "Think you can handle things here?"

He grinned. "I got this. You go do what you need to do. Tell Kasper I say hi."

We drank together for another hour, reliving some of the memories we had from the time when Archie Kasper had lived in Singletree, Maryland with us, and then I crashed in Wade's guest room. When I woke to the sun streaming through the big windows overhead, I was filled with a sense of hope.

I was about to have an adventure.

Chapter Two

AUBREY

"Who was that?" I asked my brother, tossing a piece of popcorn at him across the living room of the shabby hotel suite we'd turned into our new home.

He grinned at me, his dark eyes flashing. "Hooch hookup."

"Let me just get out my Archie dictionary," I said, pretending like I was reaching beside me for something. "What the hell does that mean?"

"Do you remember the Blanchard twins from back when we lived in Singletree?"

"You mean podunk, Maryland?" A shudder went through me. That had not been my favorite place to live on the long list of not great places my dad's naval career had taken us.

"Yes," Archie said, ignoring my distaste.

"No. I don't remember them."

"Twins? Tall guys?"

I totally remembered them. They were both cute, in a high school guy kind of way. Of course, I'd been a kid, so any and all attraction I felt was both exaggerated and futile. "Okay, yes, I guess so."

"Well, they're pretty well known now because they run their family distillery, and they've expanded it a ton. So I called them to see if they want to come hook up our liquor program here."

"Liquor program?" I looked around. So far, the old resort our insane uncle had left us consisted of a main hotel building so run down it might have been legally condemnable, and two ancient chair lifts practically falling down the side of a mountain outside. "For when we give up on this ridiculous plan and decide to just drink ourselves silly?"

My brother shook his head. "Nope. You just focus on getting that yurt situation pulled together. I'm going to have a functional bar here soon, and people are going to travel just to visit it."

"Why would anyone travel to visit a bar when they can get a beer on any corner in any town?"

"Because Kasper Ridge Resort is going to be a destination."

That was a little hard to imagine, considering the place qualified only as the kind of destination most folks would flee, but my brother had been known to accomplish some amazing feats.

"Okay," I said. "So, these guys are coming out here?" I pretended that the idea of seeing the grown-man version of my childhood crushes wouldn't be a big deal.

"Only Wiley. And go easy on him. Sounds like he just ended an engagement."

I wasn't sure what to make of this news. I felt a little douse of disappointment for no reason I could put my finger on. Was I sad that he hadn't come chasing after the twelve-year old sister of a guy he'd known in high school to propose to me instead? Or was I excited at the prospect of meeting Wiley Blanchard again in my decidedly more adult form?

"Okay. When's he getting here?"

"A week, I think. So we'd better get another one of the rooms cleaned up for him."

"Roger that."

I spent the next week supervising assembly of the yurts I'd ordered—high-end tent-like structures being built behind the main lodge on wooden platforms. The idea was to attract the glamping set up here for a high-end adventure vacation during the summer while construction on the main resort was underway.

The yurts were super cool, with king-sized beds and little bathrooms set up inside. They sat around a central fire pit and outdoor kitchen area where we'd serve food and drinks.

During the day, I'd lead hikes and rock-climbing outings in the mountains around us, which I'd been exploring with my uncle since I was a little kid. Archie hadn't been part of much of that—he always had his head buried in some model plane kit. All he ever wanted to do was fly a plane. He got his wish, but now I wondered if he would have been better off learning to tie rock climbing knots with me.

We didn't talk about the crash that ended Archie's military career.

And that was fine with me, I guessed. As long as my brother was happy. And for whatever crazy reason, it seemed like this rundown resort project was making him happy.

"Hey," Archie called as I passed through what would one day be a high-end lobby on my way back out to the yurts. "Look what I found up in Wiley's room."

He held up a piece of crumpled parchment, and I knew immediately what it was.

"Another piece of the map? Where was it?"

"Under a floorboard."

"You're pulling up the floorboards now? I thought we were just tidying a bit for this guy."

"No, it was already halfway up. I was trying to push it back into place, and the edge of this was poking out."

"Lemme see." I grabbed for the map, but Archie held it over his head. I was only five two, so this was his favorite way of keeping things from me. I huffed out a breath. "You're going to regret that."

"Oh yeah?"

My brother had a really short memory. Every time he did this, I kneed him in the nuts and he immediately crumpled, basically handing me whatever he was keeping from me. You'd think a guy would remember something like that.

"Yeah," I told him, lifting my knee hard and reminding him why holding stuff out of my reach never ended well for him.

As he lay clutching himself and moaning, I investigated the map. We had two other pieces of it, one of which had been delivered with the news that we'd inherited this old place. The second piece had been waiting for us in a shoebox, along with a letter explaining that Uncle Marvin had hidden some important treasure somewhere in the surrounding mountains, and that we'd need to locate it to understand the true nature of our inheritance.

The map was a mess of dotted lines, sketched-in trees and buildings, roads, and elevation marks. It didn't make any sense yet, but if we kept finding pieces, it would soon.

The newest piece didn't offer much. "It's like a corner or something," I complained. "Almost totally blank."

"Left side," Archie moaned, and I looked to see that there was an interesting symbol there on the left side.

"What is that? Like a cross?"

Archie was getting to his knees. "Yeah, I think so."

"Was Uncle Marv super religious?"

"You spent more time with him than I did," my brother said, glaring at me. "That hurt. A lot."

"Don't hold things over your head and leave your nuts exposed."

"I didn't know leaving my nuts exposed was something I needed to worry about when I'm at home with my family."

"The best offense is a good defense, I reminded him."

"You're insane. Don't ever do that again. I might like to have children someday."

"Scary thought," I said, poking him in the ribs as he stood.

"Put that with the other pieces, okay? I think I hear a car."

Archie headed out the front door, and I ran the map up the stairs to the suite. Not because he'd told me to, but because from there I could get a better view of the circular drive out front, where a dark green Jeep was pulling in.

I watched as Archie greeted the man who stepped out of it. Wiley Blanchard had definitely grown up, I thought.

And out. He was about six-feet-four inches of broad-shoul-dered country-boy muscle, from the looks of it. I wondered if he still had that cute southern twang. Marylanders didn't have a strong accent, but I'd noticed it when I'd lived there. And on a man that looked like Wiley Blanchard did now? I thought it just might be lethal.

Chapter Three

WILEY

The resort, if you could really call it that, was something. Just not something most folks would call a resort. It was huge, for starters, and it looked like it was well past its prime. The thing stood three stories, nestled into a flat spot atop a winding curvy road that had taken me about four hours from Denver. The rustic structure had definitely seen brighter days. The circular drive was in decent shape, but the structure that had clearly stood over it at some point, shielding arrivals from whatever weather the Rockies had in store, had crumpled and sat in a piled heap off to one side, the columns still standing in place to hold up the sky overhead.

"Wiley Coyote!" A familiar voice called, and Archie Kasper appeared, loping from the darkened double doors of the big building.

"Hey man," I said, slapping him on the back. "You look good. Being out of the military is working for you."

"Yeah." A cloud passed over his face and I realized it was probably the wrong thing to say, but we'd have to get past that kind of awkward if we were going to be together all summer.

"Love what you've done with the place," I said.

He turned to look at the dilapidated resort with me and laughed. "Yeah, I know it doesn't look like much right now. But the bones are good. I'm pretty confident this is going to be something great."

"Cool," I said. I was up for an adventure. The flight and long drive up the mountain had given me time to think, and it felt like this was a next phase in my life. A new door opening. To reveal a really run-down hotel.

"Come on in, I'll show you around. And you can say hi to Aubrey." He grabbed a duffel bag I handed him as I pulled it from the car. "You remember my sister, right?"

"Kind of? She was like twelve, I think."

"Yeah, she was twelve. But now she's twenty-three." He led me through the big doors of the building and into a high-ceilinged space that must once have been beautiful. I could see how it might be again, with the right attention.

"This is all yours?" I asked him as he led me to one side of two winding staircases that met in the center behind the reception desk. "Yeah," he said. "It's either a blessing or a curse, I guess. But it came right when I really needed a focus, and so I'm going with blessing."

"You guys both staying here then?"

"Yeah, Aubrey was just finishing school, and instead of looking for a job, I convinced her to come back here. Wasn't a hard sell. She's always loved it here."

We reached the top of the stairs and headed into a hallway where half the carpet had been pulled from the floor and lay in tatters at the sides of the wide space. Ornate chandeliers lit the way down the long corridor, half the bulbs dark.

"Set you up in a room down here," Archie told me, leading me along the hall. Eventually, we stopped outside a large set of double doors. "This room is on the corner. Awesome views. Might still need a little work, but it'll be good for now, I think." He unlocked the door and handed me the old-fashioned metal key as we stepped inside.

I dropped my bag and walked into the space. This room had clearly been one of the higher-end accommodations. I saw three doorways leading off from the central space, which held a long dining table, a living area with low couches situated in front of sweeping windows looking out on the mountains, and a little kitchenette. "Nice," I said, grinning at my friend. "This is the nicest place I've ever stayed, if you don't count the holes in the furniture and the way the rug is kind of half-eaten over there in the corner."

"One day, my friend, we'll get thousands a night for this room." Archie smiled, and I could almost picture the place fixed up.

As I looked around my new home, which was a two-bedroom suite with a king-sized canopy bed in one room and a second space that had been turned into some kind of office, I felt a sense of rightness. The lingering sadness over Amberlynn and her absence from my life fluttered around inside me, but those things were overshadowed by the potential of a new adventure, and this was certainly going to be an adventure.

"Hey," a voice came from the doorway to the suite, and I turned to find a woman leaning against the frame, her arms crossed over her chest and a little smile on her face.

"Hey," I managed, though something about the way she gazed at me had me a little off balance.

"You remember my sister, Aubrey." Archie walked over and pulled the woman into a rough hug and then proceeded to give her a noogie. She responded by performing some kind of maneuver I'd only seen in kung fu movies, but it happened fast, and she executed it so adeptly that Archie was on his back on the floor in a matter of seconds.

"Remind me never to challenge you to a fight," I said. I reached out to shake her hand over Archie's gasping body.

"Don't manhandle me, and we should be fine," she said. Her voice was raspy but feminine, and I was intrigued by her total self-possession, her clear take-no-prisoners attitude. She wore tight jeans tucked into sturdy-looking hiking boots and a fitted V-neck T-shirt that revealed some intriguing curves beneath the hard exterior. Her hair was obviously very long, but had been braided into a complicated arrangement, leaving just the end of the braid to hang over one shoulder in a golden-brown rope.

"My sister," Archie said, once he managed to get to his feet again. "The best wingman and bodyguard I've ever had." He rubbed his low back and shook his head. "You'd never know it to look at her, but she'd give John Cena a run for his money in the ring."

Aubrey grinned at this with what I thought was pride, and I made a mental note not to piss her off.

"Nice to see you again," I told her. I didn't really remember the scrappy little sister of my high school friend, but if I'd had any idea what she was going to grow into, I might have taken more notice. She wasn't pretty in a traditional way, but there was something so sure and put together about her that you couldn't help but admire her. A flicker of interest glowed to life inside me—something I barely recognized after being with the same woman my whole life.

"Archie says you're going to get us all set up in the bar," she said. "Care to see what you're working with?"

"Yeah, I brought a case of Half Cat to get us started," I said. "Show me the way."

"A case?" Archie said, leading us out of my new room. "That'll be enough for the three of us, but we're going to need more when we get this place open."

"Not a problem," I assured him, and I followed them down the long hallway, doing my best to keep my eyes off my friend's little sister's very tight, very perky ass.

Chapter Four

AUBREY

Crap on a Pringle. The grown-up version of Wiley Blanchard was hotter than anything my pre-pubescent mind could have imagined. And then I went and flipped my brother to the ground within three seconds of meeting the guy. I'm sure he saw me as womanly and attractive now. He was probably scared to death of me, like every other guy I'd ever been interested in.

So I came off a little . . . gruff.

I'd had to protect myself most of my life. Once Dad and Mom were gone, Archie was all I'd had. And he was off flying jets all over the place, so I learned how to take care of myself. It had definitely come in handy once or twice in college.

"Bar's in here," Archie said, leading us back through the lobby. I was filled with equal parts pride and shame as we showed Wiley our new home. It was going to be incredible, I knew it was. But right now, it took a special kind of person to see the glowing jewel shining from within the dusty, dilapidated trappings of the resort.

"Shit, yeah," Wiley said, stepping into the bar and looking around with appreciative eyes. It was a western-style tavern with a huge, long oak bar spanning one full side of the room.

"Cool, right?" My brother asked him, crossing his arms and standing in the center of the room as Wiley slowly made a tour.

The walls were covered with photographs, most of them black and white and all of them showing someone famous standing somewhere in this very space along with Uncle Marvin. There were movie stars and socialites, cowboys and athletes. I watched Wiley take in the photos of Marilyn Monroe, John Wayne, Elvis, and Mohammad Ali. Each one was signed by the celebrity, and in every one, Uncle Marvin stood there grinning, that mysterious gleam in his eye.

"These are worth a fortune right here," Wiley pointed out, scanning the photos.

"Probably," Archie agreed. "What do you think of the bar?"

Wiley walked the length of it, running a hand over the brass rail at its edge. I watched the big strong hand caress the bar top and an unwanted shiver of desire swept through me. What would that hand feel like running along my arm? Up my side?

He lifted the door and moved behind the bar, walking back toward me on the other side. "It's perfect," he said. He nodded to the dusty window at one side of the room, which let in very little light through the years of buildup on its surface. "Get that puppy cleaned up, get some natural light in here, shine things up . . ." I could almost see the bar taking a new shape inside his head. He grinned at both of us. "Yeah."

"Awesome," Archie said. "Come see the rest of the place."

We toured Wiley through all three floors and both wings of the massive old hotel, pointing out the work we'd already commissioned and asking his opinion on many of the things left to be approached. Then we headed out back, past the wide sweeping space that would be a deck that Archie promised would one day soon hold legions of travelers, lounging around fire pits and kicking back with a drink while overlooking the incredible vistas of the Rocky Mountains. We followed a rough trail through the trees and around a little bend to a wide clearing, hopefully far enough from the resort to provide some sanctuary when construction was underway over there.

"And this," Archie announced, "is Aubrey's baby."

We stood between the four big yurts I'd had constructed, near the enormous round fire pit we'd built from long wide stones. High-end Adirondack chairs with plush cushions dotted the open spaces, and men were at work already building the outdoor kitchen, which was set off to one side. It was mostly an enormous barbecue along with a built-in oven and refrigeration unit, along with another bar, tucked into a log structure that had retractable walls. We could lock it up at night, and keep it open and staffed during the day, serving food and drinks to glampers on demand.

Wiley stepped up onto one of the low platforms where the yurts had been set up and walked into one, glancing behind him at me with a grin.

From inside, his voice rang out, "Holy shit, this is nicer than my house."

"Right?" I asked, forgetting my strange nervousness around him and following him inside. Archie had been skeptical about my glamping plan, and the appreciation for its realization was rewarding.

"Seriously, this place is nice." Wiley turned and shot that high-wattage smile at me, practically melting my clothes from my body.

I caught his eyes, my cheeks burning hot, and we held a look that felt like it might set the whole place on fire before I ripped my gaze away. "That was the idea," I said, attempting to gather my thoughts in the aftermath of whatever had just rippled through the air between us. Could Wiley feel it too? "We want to offer a really high-end mountain resort experience, even though we are still in the process of getting the high-end mountain resort set up. So we went for a slightly different angle. It might not attract the same level of travelers, but people with money who like a unique experience instead of the same exact five-star accommodations over and over might appreciate it."

Wiley was nodding, walking around the space. "It's bigger than it looks," he said. "And this bed . . ." he trailed off, shaking his head in clear amazement at the uber plush king-sized beds I'd outfitted the spaces with.

Watching him run his hand over the end of the dove gray duvet had me imagining hurling myself at him, knocking him to his back on top of that bed and seeing what might happen next. But my instincts when it came to men were generally not on target. I was the friend, not the seductress. And most guys didn't appreciate being tackled.

So I stood my ground.

He explored the sitting area off to one side, poked his head into the bathroom—complete with rain shower—and gazed out the windows at the views of the forest on one side and towering mountains on the other.

"This is really cool," he said, coming back to the center of the room to stand beside me. "When do the first guests arrive?"

"Not really sure," I told him. "We need to get some kind of site up to advertise, and then we'll have to staff it.

For now, it's just the three of us here, but hopefully soon this place will be rocking."

Wiley smiled as I said this and his eyes remained on my face after I'd finished speaking, trailing from my eyes down to my lips and then slowly back up. His eyes were a golden brown that matched his hair, and there was a glint of fun in them, even as they darkened with something I couldn't quite name, or didn't dare to hope for.

I cleared my throat, uncomfortable under his scrutiny, but also dreading the moment it would end. I couldn't remember the last time a man had looked at me this way. Like he was hungry, and I was the only thing that might offer satisfaction. It sent anticipatory tingles shooting through me.

"It's really nice to see you again, Aubrey," Wiley said.

The air inside the yurt suddenly felt stifling. "You too," I managed, risking a look back into those eyes and regretting it instantly as everything inside me begged to get closer to the big magnetic force in front of me.

"You guys get lost in there?" Archie called through the door, breaking the spell.

I spun, heading for the entrance. "Nah, we're coming." I needed to get away from the pull of Wiley's gaze, his presence.

I had to be imagining the way he was looking at me, right? I was just his friend's little sister. Or at least that was the relationship I was used to. But I wasn't twelve anymore.

Chapter Five

The three of us had dinner together, sitting around the little table up in Aubrey and Archie's suite, which was clearly something close to the presidential suite, or the king's rooms, or whatever name would indicate that the place was meant to be the pimp daddy of hotel rooms.

They'd fixed up their own rooms as much as they'd been able to prior to bringing in the heavy guns, which I understood were going to start rolling in within the next few weeks, and though we grilled our own food out on their sweeping balcony under the watchful gaze of the mountains around us, it was a lot like eating in a five-star restaurant. Not that I'd done a hell of a lot of that.

"You know, when you guys get this place fixed up, it'll be way too nice for me to stay here," I told them, swallowing a delicious bite of steak.

"Well, us too," Archie pointed out. "Not like we grew up staying in places like this."

"Well, I mean, we kind of did," Aubrey corrected. "We stayed in a place just like this. With Uncle Marv."

I glanced at her, something I'd been trying to stop doing because every time I looked at her the most uncomfortable thoughts flew through my head, and more than once I'd been fighting a pretty embarrassing physical reaction to her too. "What was it like back then?"

"It wasn't all that long ago," Aubrey pointed out. "I'm only twenty-three."

"Right." I took a sip of the water in front of me, working to keep my reactions to her under control. Aubrey had turned into a gorgeous woman, and I was trying hard to keep my head right around her. She was Archie's little sister, after all. And I was here because he'd invited me. To set up a liquor program and run the bar—not to take advantage of his spitfire little sister. And besides, I'd broken off a four-year long engagement about a week ago. My head and my heart needed time to process that, didn't they?

But as Aubrey talked about growing up, spending her summers here with her uncle even as the place was beginning to decay around them, I couldn't help the way I felt. Like she was the most interesting woman I'd ever met. Like there was something so compelling and attractive about her that it might be physically impossible to be around her all summer and not get to touch her, to hold her, to see what it would be like to pull all that energy close and try to channel it toward me.

"I guess it was possible he was losing it even then, and my parents just didn't really know because they never came up here."

"So every summer they shipped us off to hang out in a dilapidated hotel with our nutty uncle," Archie said.

"He was your dad's brother?" I asked.

Aubrey shook her head, taking a sip of wine. "Dad's uncle, actually. He was our great uncle."

"The guy was as old as dirt."

"Didn't stop him from climbing around these hills like a kid," Aubrey pointed out.

"That's what I'm worrying about," Archie said, almost under his breath.

"What do you mean?" I asked. There'd been an undercurrent of something between the siblings, something to do with this project, and I hadn't figured out what it was. "Why would that matter now?"

They exchanged a look, and Aubrey squared her shoulders at her brother, like she was prepared to fight him if they didn't agree on whatever thing they were silently debating. "Just tell him," Aubrey suggested.

Archie leaned back in his chair and a half-smile took over his lips. "If you don't already think we're nuts, you will now."

"You guys have been to Singletree. Most people don't

know nuts, but you have to keep in mind the place I grew up," I pointed out.

"This is true," Aubrey said. "Do they still change the name at Christmas to Christmas Tree?"

I grinned. "No one gets mail in December. Drives the post office crazy."

"And is your ex-future-mother in law still sharing her house with a bunch of rodents in hats?" Archie asked.

I stiffened, a little protective of my Singletree family. "They're chinchillas," I told him. "And they're very well behaved. It's not their fault Lottie likes to dress them up." The free-range chinchillas were harmless, really. Unless you wanted to display a gingerbread house or left a bowl of rolls on the counter.

"All right. You have some experience in nuts," Archie agreed.

"Uncle Marv left us a treasure map," Aubrey blurted out, grinning.

"Like a pirate map? With an X and everything?" I asked, intrigued.

"Not quite," Archie said, leaning in and lowering his voice as if there might be someone else around to hear. "There's a poem, first of all. That's what he left us in the will. And the poem came with one piece of the map. It's supposed to lead us to the others and ultimately the treasure, but we've been getting lucky so far and just kind of discovering pieces of the map."

"Seriously?" I asked, marveling at what sounded like a really cool adventure. "That's like a real-life escape room or something."

"Yeah, but there are no hints," Aubrey pointed out.

"What's the treasure?" I asked, imagining a huge chest buried somewhere on the property.

Archie shrugged. "We don't know for sure. But the guy had a fortune at one point, and he didn't trust banks or accountants, so he had all kinds of weird ways of hiding his money."

This whole conversation was fascinating. The idea of a treasure hunt had me excited in a way I didn't think I had been since I was a little kid. "So you're figuring it all out?"

Aubrey laughed. "Not really. We haven't had a ton of time, trying to get this place back together so we can haul it out of debt."

That didn't sound good. "So you kind of need to find the treasure, and you're hoping it's cold hard cash."

"Or something valuable at least," Archie said. "But knowing our uncle, it's probably something bizarre that had value to him alone."

"Or it's cash," Aubrey suggested, looking hopeful.

"We do think the bulk of his fortune didn't convey with the will," Archie agreed. "That it's here somewhere. If not hidden at the end of the map, then just stashed somewhere in the building. That's why we're only bringing in contractors who will sign some paperwork our lawyer drew up."

"Paperwork?" I tried to picture your average plumber being presented with a complicated legal document and asked to sign before he could get the pipes working up here again.

"If they find anything in the course of their duties here, they get ten percent if they present it to us immediately. But we'll prosecute to the fullest extent of the law if they keep it from us."

We finished up our meal and took some of the Half Cat whiskey I'd brought out to the hot tub they'd gotten running on their deck. As I slipped into the hot bubbling water, I stared around myself, marveling at how much my life had changed in a short period of time. The dark green of the trees and the towering mountains off to one side gave me the sense of being very small, and of the world and my life stretching ahead of me being much bigger than it had felt in Maryland.

I let my eyes search the scenery, partly because it was breathtaking, and partly to keep them from falling on the beautiful woman sitting across from me in the hot water with her hair piled up on top of her head.

Every time Aubrey reached for her glass, her top half popped out of the bubbling water and I had to fight not to stare. She wore a red bikini in a sporty design. Not the triangle top thing that Amber had liked, the one that was made mostly for sitting still. Aubrey's suit made me think of beach volleyball players—it was made to move in. Practical, but still ridiculously sexy.

And the soft swell of her breasts was almost more than I could take.

When Archie announced he was going to turn in for the night and left the two of us alone beneath the warm water and the cool Colorado sky, I realized two things:

He trusted me with his little sister. And he absolutely shouldn't have.

Chapter Six

AUBREY

I wanted Wiley in a way I didn't think I'd wanted anyone before. I didn't know if it was because of our previous relationship—if you could even call it that—when we'd been young. Or if it was something completely independent of the vague familiarity I felt around him.

But when he'd walked across our deck in a low-slung pair of swim trunks and whipped his shirt off over his head to reveal the most perfectly chiseled set of pecs and abs I'd ever seen, I'd realized that this summer was going to be sheer torture. How could I be around a guy I found this insanely attractive and not go insane myself?

And the way he looked at me . . . I suspected he might have at least a vague interest in me too.

So when Archie said goodnight, I figured we might as well get this out of the way. I wasn't above making the first move, and if Wiley rejected me, I'd put the whole thing behind me, and we could get on with the business at hand.

The night was sliding down the sky around us, casting darkness to the distant reaches of the deck, and the lights beneath the water glowed in an otherworldly way. It felt like we were alone in the universe, Wiley and me, every-thing else drowned out by the sound of bubbles, the feel of hot water on my limbs, and whiskey sliding down my throat.

"So," I began, not exactly sure where women who were good at seduction might instruct me to start this effort.

Wiley's eyes found mine and a slow smile spread over his lips. "So," he repeated.

"Do you think you're going to like it here, Wiley?" I watched him as he watched me, saw the way his lids hooded his dark eyes, the way he licked his lips before he answered.

The smile faded a bit. "I guess that depends," he said.

"On what?"

"On a few things," he said. "Mostly on whether I'm going to be able to keep reminding myself that you're my buddy's sister."

I let that sink in. There was only one reason I could think of why he'd need to remind himself of that. I set down my glass on the edge of the tub and slowly crossed the distance between us, crouching in the hot water just in front of Wiley, watching him.

"Is that hard to remember?" I asked, my voice almost a whisper, just loud enough to be heard over the bubbles.

A big hand came up and Wiley mopped his face as if he was trying to ground himself, keep himself in check. He let out a long breath and then answered, "yeah. Sometimes it is."

"Like now?" I asked sliding closer, letting my hands come to rest on his outer thighs beneath the water.

He hissed in a breath, his eyes hot on mine. "Yeah, like now."

I slid my hands up his legs, letting them ghost up his abdomen as I moved closer still, straddling him and coming to rest on his knees, my hands on his chest. His skin was slick and his chest was firm beneath my fingers, the ridges of his body doing things to my insides that had me clenching muscles I'd ignored far too long.

Those eyes were gleaming now, dark with what I suspected was desire, and his breath was coming faster, but he didn't lay a hand on me. "Aubrey," he said, his voice a strained whisper. "Your brother is my friend."

"I'm your friend," I pointed out, sliding a little closer down his thighs.

His hands found my waist beneath the water and the last of my worry that he'd reject me dissolved in the silky hot water around us. "I don't think Archie would want—"

"Would you like to know what I want?" I asked him,

leaning in close enough that my breasts ghosted against his chest, making his grip tighten reflexively on my hips.

"God, yes," he groaned.

I slid closer, my center coming to rest against the hard length in his trunks. Wiley bit his lip, his thumbs beginning to trace up and down my ribcage as I leaned into him.

"I want to feel you inside me. On top of me, beneath me. I want to see how much of you I can take in my mouth. I want to watch you lose control, and I want you to make me scream your name." The grip on my hips was like a vise now, and I felt the iron rod beneath me stiffen further.

"Shit," Wiley breathed, and I could see him fighting for control. He let out a strained breath and then tore his gaze from mine, glancing back toward the sliding door to the suite I shared with Archie. "Your brother—"

"Isn't my keeper," I told him, letting my hands wander up his chest, my fingers playing with the soft hair there, and one hand tracing up his neck, along the edge of his jaw.

"But if he looked out here," he said, looking deliciously torn.

"He'd see me kiss you," I said, leaning down and taking his mouth with my own.

There was no hesitation in the way he kissed me back. His hands pulled me into him, making it clear that some parts of his body were definitely not torn about what should happen next in this hot tub. My mouth opened on his and our tongues met, thrusting and sliding as our bodies aligned and I felt the sweet pressure that came from pressing my chest to his, that sense of being met, being matched.

We kissed for a long time, me sitting on Wiley's lap out under the starry sky. His hands roamed my body and I felt like some kind of sex goddess, having seen what I wanted and claimed it. But we couldn't have sex in the hot tub with my brother right inside. Plus, I wasn't sure that was totally sanitary, and we'd probably want to sit in it again.

Besides, I wasn't quite that easy. I knew Wiley wanted me, but I thought maybe he should work a little harder for it. And a niggling fear in the back of my mind told me I might not be able to walk away from a simple fling. The crush I'd had as a kid was still there, only it had very adult ideas about the kinds of relationships that were possible now that I was grown. And though I'd had some one-night stands in my day, a summer entanglement would probably only leave me sad when Wiley went back to Maryland.

Despite every cell in my body screaming at me to stay in his arms, take things to the next level, I pulled away.

Wiley released me as soon as I began to move back.

I retook my position across from him, trying not to take any pleasure in the confused and very lusty look on his face.

"That was nice," I told him.

He grinned. "Uh, yeah. It was."

"Maybe you're right, though."

He looked dazed. "About what?"

"My brother. The wisdom of us getting involved that way."

He nodded, clearly thinking about this. "Yeah," he said. "I just got here. And we have all summer." Disappointment washed through me. What had I wanted him to say?

"Right. No need to rush things."

"Of course," he said, though his face was saying something else. He stood and climbed out of the hot tub, and my eyes glued themselves to his perfect body as he wrapped a towel around his hips.

I pressed the button to stop the bubbles and climbed out too, grabbing a towel and drying myself off, feeling awkward beside him.

"So the way I see it," he said slowly, like he was figuring things out as he spoke. "Either we put this off, both of us wondering what it might be like all summer and maybe me going back to Maryland never having found out what you taste like."

A shiver went through me at that.

"Or," he said, drawing the word out. "You can show me around that yurt we were looking at earlier."

I'd never have imagined that the hottest proposition I'd ever get would include the word 'yurt,' but there it was.

"Yurt," I confirmed.

"Meet you there?" he asked.

"Ten minutes," I said.

We went back inside, and Wiley let himself out as everything in me jumped and skittered in anticipation. I rinsed off quickly and then pulled on a soft sundress, not bothering to put anything under it. I let my hair down to fall over my shoulders in waves, and swiped the tiniest bit of gloss over my lips. Then I pulled a few condoms out of the bottom drawer in the bathroom and let myself out of the suite to meet Wiley.

Chapter Seven

WILEY

I sprinted through the shower in my room, hopefully standing still long enough to rinse the chlorine from my skin. But I was too turned on to really focus on the task.

Kissing Aubrey was like . . . well, I didn't know what it was like. But after four years of engagement and almost eight years of dating Amberlynn before that, it was unlike anything I could remember.

I didn't want to compare them. I loved Amberlynn, and I'd never cheated on her or given her any reason to doubt my devotion. But it had been a long time since that sizzling heat had danced in the air between us, and I wasn't sure it had ever been anything like the frenzy inside me when Aubrey had slid onto my lap, those blue eyes meeting mine. Not to mention her lips.

We'd made out like teenagers in the hot water, and my

body was coming to life as if it had been in hibernation until now.

I wasn't going to consider questions of right or wrong. My innate loyalty to my hometown and the people I loved there weren't part of this. I was a free man, I reminded myself. And Aubrey was a willing adult woman. The only person besides her that I should probably have been thinking about as I pulled on a pair of jeans and a T-shirt was Archie. And that was pretty simple, really. I didn't want to.

The hallway outside our rooms was dark, as was the first floor of the hotel, something I imagined wouldn't be the case when there were real guests staying here, but I could understand the desire to save on electricity for now. Still, the enormous lobby was murky, and I actually got turned around for a few minutes before finding my way outside.

The moon was high and full, and once my eyes had become accustomed to the darkness, I found the trail behind the hotel easily, the worn earth bright against the darker ground around it. I moved quickly, some innate part of me acknowledging that I was a relatively defenseless human wandering alone in a place where predators prob-ably roamed at night. I knew there would be mountain lions here, and possibly bears, and for a moment I found myself worrying about Aubrey. We should have come out together instead of meeting at the yurt. I hadn't thought about it because, hell, I'd been here less than twenty-four hours.

But as I turned the last bend in the trail, I was greeted but a soft golden glow coming from one of the big domed tents, and Aubrey stood in the doorway. The light from behind her accentuated her figure, and she'd put on some kind of flowy little dress, leaving her athletic legs exposed. Desire shot through me again and I picked up my pace, practically sprinting the last few feet onto the deck.

Aubrey smiled at me, her blue eyes glowing in the low light on the deck. "Hi," she said, taking my hand and pulling me through the entrance.

"Hi," I managed, practically struck dumb by the way her hair fell in long waves over her shoulders, the way her pretty plump lips shone.

Her smile faded a bit, almost making her look shy, and that sent me over the edge. I tugged her hand toward me, sliding my other hand into that glorious hair and pulling her mouth toward mine. She must have pressed up onto her toes, because the pressure increased as our tongues teased and tangled, and then she pulled away. "We should close the door."

I let her go reluctantly, but my earlier thoughts of lions was enough to fuel my patience as I watched her pull the door flap shut and secure the big zipper around its perimeter.

"Come here," I said, when she turned and stood in

front of the door, looking at me with what seemed like equal parts desire and uncertainty.

Her eyes dropped to the floor and she crossed the space to where I stood in front of the huge plush bed, and with every step, my desire for her increased. She was the perfect mix of sexy and shy, self-sufficient and soft. My body responded to her so completely it was almost painful to watch her approach—that was how badly I needed to touch her.

Still, she was my buddy's little sister, and I'd hold myself back and let her guide us. There was no way I'd end tonight worrying that I might have taken advantage, or pushed her in a way she didn't want to go.

She stopped before me, her long lashes fluttering as she looked up at me, that sexy smile back on her lips. "Did you know I had a crush on you when we lived in Maryland?"

For some reason, that set fire coursing through my body. "Did you?"

She nodded, wrapping her arms around my neck. She was at least a foot shorter than I was, so I bent down to make it easier for her, and when my hands found her waist, she jumped, wrapping her legs around my waist.

"I know you can't say the same," she went on, her lips ghosting over mine and her breath warm and minty as she spoke. "I was just a kid."

"If I'd known you were going to end up this ridiculously hot woman, I would have," I told her, cringing a bit at the implication that I would have been hot for a twelve-year old. Words. Still not my strong suit. "I don't mean—" I began.

"I know what you mean," she assured me, her tongue finding a hot path from below my ear to my jaw. "It's okay."

I turned and braced one knee on the bed before me, sinking down slowly until Aubrey was beneath me, her mouth finally on mine. A low groan filled the air, and I realized it was coming from me—one of Aubrey's hands had found my throbbing erection and was rubbing along the front of my jeans between us.

I slid a hand up the smooth skin of her leg as my mouth left hers, moving to taste the silky skin of her throat. As my fingers slid higher and higher, it was Aubrey's turn to groan, and the sound ratcheted my desire up another notch.

When my fingers found her perfect round ass uncovered by any kind of panties, I knew I was a goner.

"No underwear?" I asked, my mouth trailing along her collarbone.

"No time," she said, her hands pulling at the hem of my T-shirt. I lifted my body from hers, allowing her to pull the shirt over my head, and then returned to the delightful curves I was exploring with my hands and my mouth.

Her hands slid over my skin, her nails leaving little trails of fire across my back.

I kissed the skin in the low V of the dress, and then lifted myself away from her, both to slide the dress up over her head and to admire the treasure beneath me. "Wow," I heard myself say. *Again. Words. Christ.*

"Wow yourself," she said, grinning up at me.

Her body was amazing—tight and firm, and muscular, like a gymnast's. She was compact and small, but I'd already seen the power contained in this small vessel. "You're incredible, Aubrey," I told her.

A deep blush climbed into her cheeks and she dropped my eyes.

"You don't believe it," I guessed. I shook my head. "How can a woman be as incredible as you are, and have any doubts?"

"I've never been that girl," she said simply.

"You're definitely that girl to me," I told her, dropping my head and sliding down her tight little body to kiss her navel, and finally, to let my tongue trace through the wetness at her center.

"Oh God," she moaned, breathy and deep.

I kissed and sucked, adding my fingers to the equation, beginning to learn Aubrey's body. I paid attention to what she liked, and what didn't seem to do anything for her, changing pressure and tempo as her moans suggested I should. When she let go, surprise coloring her soft moans of pleasure, I felt like I'd won some kind of sexual Olympics.

I kissed my way back up her torso, taking time to admire and kiss each small breast before taking her lips with mine again.

"I have a condom," she said. "My dress . . ."

It seemed I wasn't the only one struggling with words for a change.

I stepped off the bed to retrieve her dress and took the opportunity to pull off my jeans and briefs. My erection bobbed in front of me, as if asking when it might be getting in on this action.

"Nice." Aubrey said from where she'd sat up on the bed.

I grinned at her. "Thanks." I wasn't the kind of guy who lived by the size of his dick, but it was still nice to win a lady's approval.

I moved to where she sat on the bed, placing my knees on either side of her legs. When she turned her gaze up to meet my eyes, I let my hands sink into all that soft brown hair and met her lips with mine again. Her hands, however, wrapped themselves around my cock and I thought I might lose it right there.

She rubbed and stroked, her fingers playing lightly over my skin, then tugging my balls gently and tracing lines across parts of me that were begging for more. I'd laid the condom on the edge of the bed, and I paused my assault on her lips to watch her rip it open and then roll it slowly over my aching erection.

"I want to feel all of you," she told me.

I was not going to argue.

She laid back and I braced myself above her on my elbows, nearly losing my mind as my tip found the hot inviting pulse of her entrance. And then slowly, inch by devastating inch, I slid into the hottest, wettest, tightest space I'd ever known. She was a small woman, but she took every last bit of me inside her, and I had a fleeting thought that it was like coming home, though I knew that didn't make sense.

I held still for a long moment, just letting the intense feelings roll through me, and then I began to slide slowly out, returning home over and over again as the intensity built between us.

Aubrey's eyes had slipped closed, and her mouth was opened in a beautiful little "o" as her hands gripped my back, pulling me ever closer.

"Fuck, yes," she whispered, and I could feel the shaking spasm beginning inside her. "Wiley," she breathed. "I'm gonna come."

"Come for me," I encouraged her. "I'll be right behind you."

And that was how it happened—Aubrey's moans and the tight grip her body had on my dick set me flying over the edge, and I lost myself in the perfect girl below me, the perfect connection we shared.

Chapter Eight

AUBREY

Lest you get the wrong idea, I should assure you that I'm not that kind of girl—the easy type. But I am the type who thinks that if I want something, I should go for it. And I'd never wanted a guy as much as I wanted Wiley Blanchard.

And having him?

It was better than anything I could have imagined.

Our bodies, despite our disparate heights, fit together perfectly, and he might have been the first man who could completely satisfy me. Women didn't go around measuring themselves by their channel length or anything, but I suspected mine was pretty big, not that I'd had a lot of experience in that department. I'd been with two other men, and neither had filled me enough to make me feel complete.

Or maybe it was less about Wiley's size and more about who he was.

"Holy shit," I breathed, as Wiley's big body covered mine. Twinkle lights glowed around the top of the yurt around us, and the night outside hummed with the sounds of the wilderness. But most of my attention was right here, with the man I knew I would fall in love with if I wasn't careful.

"Well put," Wiley said, kissing me again. He slid to one side, and his big hand came up to push my hair out of my face as he peered into my eyes. His thumb came up to stroke my cheek, and something about the way he was holding me, looking at me, made my chest warm.

We lay together until the light began to come up outside, at one point climbing beneath the exquisite sheets and blankets and snuggling together after I'd shut the lights off. But when dawn began to break, I figured we'd better head back inside.

"We need to do some laundry," Wiley pointed out as he dressed again.

"We can take care of it today," I assured him. I'd figure out how to do it so Archie wouldn't get suspicious.

We walked together back to the hulking old hotel, our hands linked and my heart feeling strangely full.

"See you later," Wiley said, as we kissed again in the hallway outside my door.

"See you—"

"There you are!" Archie's voice boomed as he thundered down the hallway toward us.

I looked around, my brain taking a moment to catch up. He wasn't in our room. He wasn't asleep.

"Uh, morning," I said, stepping away from Wiley as if that would make it less obvious what we'd been up to.

"One night, huh, Blanchard? You didn't last one night around my sister." His words were angry, but his expression wasn't.

"You mad?" I asked, feeling very much like the little sister in that moment.

"You're adults," he said.

Wiley blew out a long breath and wrapped a big hand around the back of his neck, his eyes dropping. I sensed he was searching for words. "Kasper," he began finally. "I feel like I should apologize or something, but I don't think I can."

"No?" Archie asked, looking a little confused.

"No. Look," he said, taking my hand again. "I know Aubrey is your sister. And I know my own situation here is . . . well, temporary probably. And that most guys wouldn't want their sister involved with someone who'd just ended a long relationship."

My brother was nodding, but I was hanging on Wiley's every word.

"The thing is," he said, pausing again. "Well, I think there's something here." He motioned between us. "I'm not one of those guys, the kind that takes advantage just because he can. And I don't have one-night stands or run around. It's just not me."

"What do you mean 'something'?" I asked, unable to help myself.

Wiley turned to me, his eyes meeting mine and then dropping to the ground. "I know we've had one night. And that's nothing to base anything on probably, and maybe I'm not a good judge of this kind of stuff. But I like you. A lot. And I have this feeling. I mean . . . if I'm here all summer, maybe we have time to see what this is?"

"Kind of fast forwarded the thing, don't you think?" Archie asked.

"I don't always do things right," Wiley admitted. "But I'd never hurt you," he assured me. "Would you maybe want to be my date for the summer?"

I didn't even have to think about it. "Yes," I said, the grin stretching my cheeks as I tightened my grip on his hand.

"For fuck's sake, this isn't the prom," Archie said, shaking his head. But a glance at his face told me he wasn't really upset. "So I'm gonna be the third wheel all summer, that's what you're telling me?"

I shrugged, and then wrapped an arm around my brother. "No," I told him. "You'll still be my big brother."

He sighed, but seemed to accept this, and my heart

swelled inside my chest. I felt happier than I could remember being in . . . well, forever.

"Listen, the entire reason I was up at dawn and even noticed you were gone was because the contractor called. They had to shuffle some things, and so construction in the lobby and restaurant is starting today."

Almost as if brought forth by his pronouncement, the sound of an enormous engine began to grow louder outside.

"That'll be some of the equipment," Archie said. "Get on some work clothes. Shit's about to get real."

And for the next week, shit did get real. Fast.

Nights were my favorite time—when the drills and hammering quieted down and the three of us made dinner and then sat out in the hot tub on the deck. I spent most of my nights in Wiley's bed—since my brother knew, there was no point in pretending we didn't want to be together.

And it felt so simply right, I decided not to question the speed with which it had happened.

We were sitting in the hot tub late one evening when Archie stood and faced us both. "So I have something to tell you," he began, and I stiffened. This was weird.

"What?" I demanded.

"I've been dying to tell you all day," he said. "But wanted to wait until it was quiet around here."

Wiley and I were both tense with anticipation. Our lives here were so routine, this "something" seemed both exciting and vaguely threatening.

"The guys uncovered something today during demolition on the third floor rooms."

My heart rate sped up. "What?"

"You'll have to see it for yourself," he said. "Come on."

We all hopped out of the tub and dried off, then followed my brother to the smallest room at the end of the hall on the third floor. He switched on the lights to reveal something strange on the far wall.

"They were stripping the wallpaper," Archie said. "And they uncovered that."

He pointed to where words were scrawled in a messy cursive over the entire surface of the wall.

"Holy shit," Wiley said, sounding reverent.

"Read it," Archie encouraged us.

I read out loud, struggling a bit with some of the messier words:

A ticking clock
A lonely dock
My riches wait
Find Lola's gate.

Blood of my blood,
Heart of my heart,
Take this key.
When you're ready to start.

It was signed, "Uncle Marvin" and below the signature, a large golden key was taped to the wall.

"What?" I whined. "More riddles? I'm ready to start!"

"Yeah," Archie said, sounding a little frustrated himself. "Me too."

Wiley wrapped an arm around my shoulders and grinned down at me. "This summer's going to be the best one ever," he said. "Tomorrow, we'll start hunting for the lock that thing fits."

Archie pulled the key from the wall, inspecting it carefully in the light from above. "Hey," he breathed. "There's a symbol on this, just like that one on the map."

My heart lifted. We finally had a clue that might make some sense. "So we figure out what that symbol represents," I guessed. "First we'll need to try to understand that map better. What's this though, 'a ticking clock, a lonely dock'?"

"No idea," Archie said. "I took a picture of this with my phone, and I've got the map too."

We stood there for a long time, grinning at each other

like kids. A mystery lay before us, and for me—that, combined with the warmth of the man who stood at my side—this was going to be the best summer ever.

"Let's get some sleep," Archie suggested. "We've got a hell of a lot to do."

We did, and as I fell into Wiley's arms that night, my heart filled with joy. I was home.

If you enjoyed this story, you won't want to miss the Kasper Ridge Series! This is just the prequel to a full series of books about former jet pilots turning a not-quite-right resort into a premiere mountain destination, all set against the backdrop of Uncle Marv's treasure hunt! Read on to get a sneak peek of book one or grab it here!

USA TODAY BESTSELLING AUTHOR
Only a
FLING
DELANCEY
STEWART

Only a Fling - Chapter 1
Succeeding at Failure (Harder than it Looks)

WILL

"Do me a favor and put your phone away," Dad said the second I strode into his office.

I shoved my phone, which had been in my hand, into the pocket of my pants, simultaneously pushing down the irritation that rose inside me at the command.

Dad never changed—and it wasn't that he was angry or

domineering, he wasn't. He just expected people to behave a certain way, and he'd had enough experience with me to get out ahead of any disappointments I might offer him.

"I need all your attention on this rebuild on the Esplanade, Will."

For a second, hope awoke inside me, crawling from the bed where it had decided to take an indefinite slumber a long time ago.

"Yeah? I can do that." I stood taller. I'd been waiting for the opportunity to take the reins, for the moment when I'd proven myself sufficiently to my father to oversee one of the massive luxury construction projects his firm was known for. The Esplanade project was going to be huge, and I'd been second on so many projects now, it felt like maybe it was finally my turn to lead.

"Good, Markie will need your help."

"Markie?" I felt my shoulders slide back down. Of course. Markie.

I was not a Markie fan. Markie was a tough woman, good at what she did, but with a couple bags of Fritos perched high on her massive shoulders. It was pretty clear she'd had to work hard to get ahead in the male-dominated world of construction, and at this point, she assumed every guy she worked with expected her to be incompetent. She made up for it by turning herself into the kind of foreman people were afraid to piss off. Me included.

And she had a dog everyone hated but no one had the

guts to tell her was a disaster. He was a pitbull/daschund mix named Buzz, every bit as ornery and bullying as Markie.

"Yep. She's running the show. Best we've got, son. And this project is critical."

I tried to absorb that blow without letting it show on my face. And I sucked in a deep breath, girding myself for what I knew was coming out of me next. Because really, what the hell did I have to lose? "Dad? When will you trust me enough to run a project?"

Shit, I was thirty-one. The United States Navy had trusted me enough to put me in charge of a seventy-million dollar jet. But my dad wouldn't trust me to run a construction project with plenty of help. Maybe my Navy career hadn't been as glorious as his, but I'd done it, dammit. I'd flown, I'd fought, and then I'd decided it was time to move on.

Only I hadn't moved far. Dad had offered me a job at his firm, and I'd accepted. Because I'd actually hoped it might be a big enough place to grow, to finally show him I was a capable adult.

To maybe even make him proud. Of course, as soon as I'd gotten here, I'd screwed up. And it was clear Dad was never going to let me forget it.

"Not this one, son. This one is critical, and Markie's got it handled. Just be there to run defense for her, carry some of the weight when she needs you, and help manage the schedule." Dad's attention was already back on the screen in front of him. That was my cue to go.

Frustration bubbled inside me. "Dad."

He looked up again, his eyes widening slightly, like he was surprised to see me still standing there. "Will?"

"Do you think you'll ever trust me again?"

His lips tightened and I saw a muscle jump in his cheek. His steely eyes held mine for a beat, and then they softened. "Yeah," he said. "I hope so."

Hope.

He hoped he could trust me.

Someday.

I left his office and returned to my own, using every bit of restraint I had to keep from slamming the door. As I swiveled to gaze out the plate glass window, I let my mind wander back over every stupid thing I'd ever done, every act that had solidified my father's belief that I'd never be as good as him, never be ready to take on the weight of his trust.

It was a long and exhausting stroll down memory lane. But beyond all the silly shit I'd done in the Navy, the one thing I knew Dad couldn't forgive was directly related to my work here. I'd trusted someone to do what they said they would. I hadn't been a good enough leader to demand it—or to doublecheck it. And a man had almost died as a result. Since then, I'd been the most competent manager Dad had, the most engaged, the most organized.

But it still wasn't good enough. It would never be good enough.

My phone buzzed in my pocket where I'd shoved it earlier, and though my dark mood suggested I ignore it, the name on the screen piqued my curiosity. I hadn't talked to Ghost in a while, but word was going around that he'd taken on some crazy project up in the mountains in Colorado. A hotel or something.

I didn't know if running a hotel was what the guy needed, but I knew he needed something. After everything that had happened…

"Ghost," I said, hitting the speaker button and sliding my phone onto my desk.

"Fake Tom," he said, his voice warm and cheerful. It felt good to have someone address me by my callsign again. Even if I'd hated the name at first. A wash of nostalgia flooded me on hearing it on his lips. I missed it. And him. I missed all my squadron buddies. "How's it going, man?" he asked.

"Living the dream."

"I bet," he said. "Still working with your old man building those luxury condos on the beach?"

"Pretty much sums it up," I said.

He paused. "Don't sound too excited."

I wasn't going to get into it. Especially not if Ghost had just called to shoot the shit. All of us seemed to have agreed to look out for Ghost a little bit, and the last thing he needed was to hear about my petty gripes with my dad. He had bigger things to worry about.

"I heard you bought some hotel or something in the mountains," I said.

He let out a laugh. "Not exactly. My great-uncle left me the place. Me and my sister."

Ghost's sister Aubrey was a spitfire. She'd come to visit us a few times in Lemoore, and the girl was tougher than some of the drill sergeants I'd met.

"So you're living the resort life now? Rubbing elbows with the apres ski set, I guess?"

"That's the plan, but we're not there yet. Which is part of why I'm calling you."

"Aw, Ghost, you didn't just call to say hello because you missed me?"

"You know I do," he laughed. "And that is actually exactly why I'm calling you."

"I'm touched."

"In fact, I miss you so much I have an idea for you."

"Hold me. I'm frightened."

"Probably should be. Want to come up here and run the renovation on this place? I've got proposals from some top-notch crews, but I need a project manager who knows construction and can keep the whole thing on schedule. Run the show. Herd the cats." Ghost's tone was light but I sensed an undertone that hinted he might be in trouble.

I dropped into my chair, my mind whirling. "I do have

a way with puss—ahem, with cats," I joked, mostly to buy a little time to think. I knew next to nothing about the project Ghost was proposing. But I had heard him say I'd be in charge. "Tell me more."

He paused, and I sensed the bad news was coming next. "Well, I couldn't pay you much," he said, and my hopes fell. I needed an actual job. I didn't have a ton of expenses, but I did have some bills. "But I could give you free housing and a percentage."

"A percentage of...?"

"Of the Kasper Ridge Resort property."

"You're talking ownership?" Maybe Ghost was a little desperate if he was willing to pay me in equity. Still, I found myself considering it.

"I mean, I should let you know the place is in the red right now."

Of course it was. "So let me get this straight." I looked out the window at the deep indigo expanse of the Pacific stretching to the horizon and tried to imagine exchanging it for rugged mountains, pine trees. "You're offering me a low-paying job, a share of a failing business, and a shitty room in a run-down resort?"

Ghost chuckled. "I figured it was a long shot."

"I'll do it." The words were out before my brain caught up. But that was pretty much how every bad idea I'd ever acted on had come to life. Why quit now? One more way to disappoint Dad.

"Seriously?" Ghost sounded surprised, like he'd figured this was a long shot at best.

"Yeah, I'll do it. I'm sick of playing second fiddle to burly chicks in combat boots with bad breath and no sense of humor."

"That's weirdly specific."

"Send me the details."

"You got it," Ghost said. "And Fake Tom? Thanks, man."

I hung up, my insides churning with something that was either excitement or dread. I had no clue what I'd just agreed to, besides having to tolerate people calling me Fake Tom again, but even that held a certain appeal.

Maybe this was the chance I'd been waiting for. I wasn't going to let it pass me by. And when it was over? Maybe Dad would finally see me as something other than a disappointment.

Only a Fling - Chapter 2
Don't Mess with a Woman in a Hard Hat

LUCY

The grinding sound of machinery grated through the cool mountain air, sending a shiver up my spine. There were piles of dirt all around, my crew moved here and there, and Mateo was making quick work of the dig with the backhoe, meaning soon we'd be on to the more exciting parts of the build.

I lived for this chaos. There was something satisfying about the noise and the mess around me. We were driving the earth to meet our will—or the will of the ridiculously wealthy family paying us to build them a mountain home, but whatever—creating organized destruction, all in the name of accomplishment.

Just as I allowed myself a smile, the grating, sifting noise of the backhoe digging changed, replaced by a stomach-lurching, bone-shaking thump I knew too well. I heard it twice more, but kept my head down, leaning over the plans I had spread on my worktable.

The backhoe shut off and I turned to see Mateo striding toward me across the site, a grim look on his face.

"Boss. Hit rock."

I swallowed the aggravation I felt. "Bound to happen up here. We do this just about every time, right?" I shot him a confident smile.

"Thought we were gonna get lucky this time. I was more than halfway done." Mateo took off his hard hat, the crinkles around his light green eyes appearing as he returned my smile with a more doubtful one of his own. He had to peer down at me because he was at least six feet tall and I wasn't anywhere close. Somehow, though, Mateo never made me feel small. I'd known him forever, and I trusted him like a brother.

"I don't put much stock in luck. Things that come too easy aren't usually worth having, in my experience."

My friend squinted at me, the low western sun high-lighting the smears of gritty dirt on his tanned face. "Now you sound like the old man."

He was right, and my heart warmed as I thought about it. "I guess he was bound to wear off on me some time." I gazed around at the weary men surrounding me, waiting for next steps. This was only part of the crew I'd have up here once the excavation work was done. We just needed to get the site plumbed and poured before the fun part would begin, but digging in the mountains was never without adventure, and encountering rock down beneath the soil was to be expected.

"Let's call it for today. We'll get to ripping that rock early tomorrow and hopefully can get these lines plumbed starting in the afternoon. Depending on how much rock is down there."

Mateo wiped a hand across the back of his neck and pulled the hard hat from his head. "You sure, boss? Another hour of daylight here."

"It's Friday night. Go have fun, guys. But not too much. I need you tomorrow at six."

"Right," Mateo said, shaking his head. I knew his night wasn't likely to be too exciting. He was a single dad, raising a little girl on his own. "We might have time to watch *Frozen* again."

"I love that movie," I told him, earning a grin before Mateo turned and headed to his truck.

The crew slowly made their way to the vehicles parked here and there around the site. When everyone was gone, I double-checked to make sure all our equipment was secure, and then hopped into my truck. I had plans of my own tonight.

"Girl, how do you look like that when you spend all day covered in dirt and sawdust?" Bennie pulled me into a hug as I approached the little round high-top table where my girlfriends already sat with pints before them.

"Like what?" I asked innocently, batting my eyelashes.

"Shut up, you know exactly what she means," CeeCee scolded, pulling me in for a hug next.

"I like getting dressed up," I told them, smoothing the skirt of my red dress and adjusting a curl over my shoulder. "It's like exploring the two sides of my identity. Hard-assed construction boss and actual girly girl."

"Well, you do both pretty well. How's Papa?" Bennie pushed a glass and the pitcher my way, and I poured a beer after settling onto a stool.

"He's doing fine. He's busy playing poker tonight with the other old timers. I just hope he takes it easy on them this time. I don't know what I'll do if I have to listen to him complain for another month that none of his friends will speak to him."

"He's a card shark, huh?" Bennie laughed.

"He's just tricky, I guess." Papa was smart. Shrewd, maybe, was a better word. But my grandfather was also the kindest person I'd ever known, and even though I liked to complain about him to those who knew his quirks almost as well as I did, I wouldn't trade a single thing about him. Not the way he complained about my terrible cooking, or the way he stuck his nose deep into every project my construction business took on. He was a know it all maybe, but he'd earned the right—and he'd taught me literally everything I knew.

I sat back in my chair and let the tension run from my fingertips and toes, soaking in the laughter and warmth of my friends, and the people around us in the Toothy Moose, one of two local bars in Kasper Ridge. It was this place or Bud's, and you didn't go to Bud's unless you were under twenty-one and desperate to test out your fake ID, or hoping to run into someone you hadn't known since birth, since it was halfway down the mountain. The Moose was home base for most of the locals up here, and hanging out in the cozy mountain bar felt a lot like relaxing at home.

"You guys seen what's going on up at the old hotel?" CeeCee asked, her big brown eyes shining with some kind of unspilled gossip.

I sat up straighter. I knew something, but I wondered what these ladies knew. I'd been talking with Papa about it just this morning, and about the proposal I had put in at the request of the mysterious new owners.

"Did it finally collapse?" Bennie asked. It was a fair question. Kasper Ridge Resort had once been a pretty fancy ski resort, the kind of place just big enough to attract celebrities, but small enough to give them the freedom to enjoy themselves without crowds of tourists. But that was decades ago, and the guy who owned the place hadn't done a lot to keep it up in his later years. The roof that protected the receiving drive out front had collapsed a few years back, and my crew had gone in to pull the debris out of the driveway. Just in case anyone ever needed to get to the front doors again. The place was a hazard, really.

"I might have heard some things," I said. "What do you know?" Besides the request for proposals the owners had put out to construction firms as far afield as Denver, my knowledge was limited to permits filed and equipment requisitioned, and some of my guys had told me they'd helped out constructing some kind of temporary lodging structures behind the place at the start of the summer.

"That old guy that owned the place died and left it to some family of his, I guess," CeeCee said.

I frowned. The RFP had come from an LLC, so I didn't have a lot of insight into who was actually funding the job. "What kind of family?" Up here, property left to family sometimes didn't turn out well. Folks who hadn't spent years living in the mountains didn't really understand what it was to exist up here. They didn't get the culture, the harsh conditions that cropped up regularly in terms of weather, or the unspoken rules about privacy and community that mountain people just seemed to know. The last thing we needed was some slick banker type thinking he could turn the place into the next Aspen or Beaver Creek. Even though having a tourist destination up here would help keep some money coming into the local businesses, we didn't need that kind of reputation.

"A brother and sister," CeeCee said. "They're Kaspers. Mabel at the market said they came in to buy some things and told her about what they're up to." CeeCee was glowing. She was a good person—one of the best, and I'd known her since preschool, but CeeCee loved to gossip.

"Anyway," she went on, leaning forward as she got into her story. "Get this. I guess there's some kind of map or something. The old man was crazy, right? And he put together like, a treasure hunt or something, for his niece and nephew to figure out. That's why they're here."

"They came up here to nowhere ridge to go on a treasure hunt?" Bennie looked skeptical. "What's the treasure? A bunch of rocks?"

"The old guy—Marvin, I think?—he was rich, right? He ran the place when it was a fancy resort in the eighties. Famous people popping in all the time? My dad says he went there once when he was a kid and there were pictures everywhere of the guy with celebrities."

"He and Papa were friends a long time ago," I told them, remembering what Papa had told me this morning. "But they hadn't talked in years. And Marvin either ended up poor or senile, because the place is in serious need of work," I said. "But it does sound like the new owners are looking to renovate."

Both my friends were watching me now.

"You already knew," CeeCee accused, clearly disappointed that she hadn't gotten to share the juicy gossip first.

"I only know they're looking for help getting the place running again. It's a huge job."

"You putting in for it?" Bennie asked.

"I already did," I told her. "It would make the year for me, and probably next year too. Plus I could hire back all the guys I had to let go when things slowed down. And it'd be great for Kasper Ridge. All those local guys working so close to home? And think about the business the tourists would bring when the place is done." Excitement forced my words out faster than usual, and my whole body bounced in my chair. It would be a great opportunity to be involved in something that would really help our community, and would pretty much seal my own future (and Papa's).

"Your eyes are all sparkly," Bennie said. "Also, ew. Tourists."

"Tourists mean money for the town. And this job would seriously make my company," I said, allowing myself to dream a little in a way I'd told myself not to. "And if I win it, no one will ever question my abilities again. Woman or not."

"That dress says woman," CeeCee said, pointing to the flouncy red dress I'd pulled on after my shower.

"And so do those shoes," Bennie agreed. "I swear, you're the only person who wear heels up here, Luce."

"I like to dress up. And getting dressed up after work shouldn't make anyone think I'm less serious about the job while I'm there. I'm out to prove I can do both. Women can be kickass foremen."

"Forewomen," CeeCee corrected. Her forehead wrinkled. "Forepeople?"

"I'll drink to that," I said, lifting my glass. I wasn't going to think about all the jobs I'd been turned down for because of my gender. I was going to get this one.

"To the new Kasper Ridge Resort," Bennie said, joining the toast. "You better get that job so you can give us an inside peek."

We touched our glasses and drank, and then CeeCee dropped her last piece of gossip with a gleeful smile. "Guess what else I heard? The guy running the place now? The nephew? He was a Navy fighter pilot, and he's bringing up a bunch of his buddies to help. Soon Kasper Ridge will be swarming with hot men."

I shrugged. Hot men, in my experience, were not all they were cut out to be. Good for a weekend or a summer, maybe. But hot men from out of town didn't stay long in Kasper Ridge.

Grab Only a Fling here!

More Delancey

The Wilcox Wombats Series:

Book 1: The Wedding Winger

Ready for some ha ha with your hockey? The Wilcox Wombats bring the camaraderie and sense of found family you're looking for, along with snort laughs and swoons. The first book features a star winger planning for his future, but caught up in the past. When his high school torch (the smart girl who always thought he was just a dumb jock) moves back next door, he knows he's in trouble. Grab it here!

The Kasper Ridge Series:

Free Prequel: Only a Summer

Book 1: Only a Fling

Read the Kasper Ridge Series to get your fill of small town steam with plenty of humor! Former fighter pilots share deep bonds and plenty of inside jokes. Step into their world as they join together to help renovate the Kasper Ridge Resort, a dilapidated mountain property In Colorado, left as an inheritance to Ghost, one of their own. But the inheritance also comes with a treasure hunt! Each book follows a different couple but each story builds another link in the hunt, so read them in order! Start with Only a Summer, which is free! Then pick up Only a Fling here.

The Singletree Series:

Book 1: Happily Ever His

What happens when the totally normal sister of a movie starlet meets her ultimate movie star crush, only to find out he is dating her famous sister? But it gets a bit more complicated than that. Tess's sister has brought movie hottie Ryan home for her grandmother's 90th birthday to show the world how quickly she could move on after her very public divorce. The relationship is just for show… but Tess doesn't know that at first. And Gran? Is a video gaming, weed smoking, take-no-prisoners firecracker who tells it like it is. Toss in a lovesick chicken, and you're on your way to understanding what kind of series Singletree promises to be. Plan to laugh. Pick up book 1 here!

The MR. MATCH Series:

Free Prequel: Scoring a Soulmate

Book 1: Scoring the Keeper's Sister

If you enjoy a side of sports with your sexy men, and want both wrapped up in a hilarious package, then you're going to love Mr. Match. Soccer star and genius Max Winchell has discovered the formula for love and built a dating app around it. Though he keeps his identity secret, he convinces all his teammates to try it… and one after another, they fall in love. First up? Fernando "the fire" Fuerte, who shares an enemies-to-lovers romance with PR rep Erica, who happens to be his teammates twin sister. Taboo, forced proximity, and tons of witty banter up the steam in this one! Get it here!

The KINGS GROVE Series:

Book 1: When We Let Go

Coming right up, a bit of Sequoia mountain steam mixed with small town swoon! Head to Kings Grove for quirky side characters, emotional love stories, happy ever afters, and a cast you'll want to make your neighbors. Book 1 features Maddie returning to her childhood home, only to be swept off her feet by a handsome and potentially dangerous stranger. These books are steamy and engaging, with a touch of humor. Read book 1 here!

THE GIRLFRIENDS OF GOTHAM Series:

Book 1: Men and Martinis

Head to to the dot-com heyday of NYC - the late 1990s! Join Natalie Pepper as she makes her way in the big city in this Carrie Bradshaw meets Bridesmaids coming of age story. Meet the girlfriends here!

The Digital Dating Series (with Marika Ray):

Book 1: Texting with the Enemy

Looking for sweet romance with a romcom kick? That's what you get when Delancey and Marika Ray team up! In this series starter, Elle is texting a guy she isn't sure she likes, but boy does he give good text. The only problem? She's actually texting her boss since "the guy" gave her his buddy's number instead of his own. Now she's falling slowly in love with the perfect guy and can't figure out why he doesn't seem perfect in person... Needless to say, hilarity ensues. Pick it up here!

About the Author

Delancey Stewart writes books with humor, heart and heat from her adopted hometown of Denver, Colorado. She lives with her husband and two sons, and her Chocolate Labrador, Charlie Taco.

www.ingramcontent.com/pod-product-compliance
Lightning Source LLC
Chambersburg PA
CBHW070518200726
48293CB00007B/2589

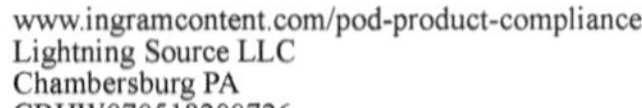